HEY, NEW KID!

Garry Kilworth

Illustrated by **Stephen Player**

mammoth

This book is dedicated to my grandson,
Christian Lillie
G.K.

To Daniel Maier
S.P.

First published in Great Britain in 1999
by Mammoth, an imprint of Egmont Children's Books Limited
239 Kensington High Street, London, W8 6SA

ISBN 0 7497 3729 8

10 9 8 7 6 5 4 3 2 1

A CIP catalogue record for this book is
available from the British Library

Printed in Great Britain by Cox & Wyman Ltd,
Reading, Berkshire

J 103 030 £ 3.99

Contents

1. Trouble in the playground

'Hey, new kid!'

Danny Bailey had been dreading these words from the moment he entered Rochford School playground. It was June 1953 and he had been to nearly a dozen schools now, though he was only thirteen years of age. The first day at a new school there was always one tough boy who shouted these words to him. Danny steeled himself for the coming encounter.

Three boys walked over. They were all wearing shirts and coarse flannel shorts. On their feet were heavy boots. These were no doubt farmworkers' sons, Rochford being a rural district in a coastal corner of Essex. The biggest boy of the three, about fourteen years of age, was sneering.

'Where have you come from, new kid?'

'Aden,' said Danny, wearily.

One of the other boys frowned. 'Where's that, Robbo?'

Danny realised that the big boy was John Robson, the youth his grandmother had warned him about. The Robsons were a tough family of four sons and three daughters, known throughout the district. They had earned their muscles on a local farm. John Robson was the youngest of the bunch, no less rugged than the older members of the family.

'Aden?' repeated Robbo. 'That's in the Middle East, you twit. Don't you know nothin', Stocky?'

Albert Stockard, another local youth.

Robbo turned again to Danny. 'Your dad in the army?'

'Air force. My dad's a sergeant in the R.A.F. Him and my mum are at a transit camp in Shropshire. We've been sent back here to get a new posting to another station.'

Robbo sneered again. 'I don't want your life history. Air force! Think you can just come here an' do what you like, eh? What school did you go to?'

'Khormaksar School.'

'Cor, mac, sir?' cried Robbo. 'What, didn't you have no overcoat?'

Stocky and the other boy laughed. There was a small crowd gathering now, of boys and girls, and laughter rippled through them. Mr Simpson was already striding towards the group, sensing trouble.

Robbo could not let it rest at that. He had an appreciative audience. 'This Aden place is in Arabia, ain't it? Say some Arab words for us, air force kid.'

Danny was about to tell him to take a running jump, when he suddenly decided to answer. '*Inta mafish muk*,' he said.

'What's that? What's that rubbish

mean?' snapped Robbo.

'It means "You have no brains",' replied
Danny, smiling.

Robbo leaped forward and aimed a
punch at Danny's nose, but Danny
stepped back, taking the blow on his
shoulder. In that instant the teacher was

amongst them. He had Robbo by the collar and was waving a finger in Danny's face. 'Break it up, you two. Both of you – report to me during first break! There'll be no fighting in the playground, you understand me? When will you ever learn, Robson?'

At that moment the bell went for assembly and the children rushed to form class lines. Danny had been to the school reception the previous afternoon and had been introduced to his form teacher. He knew which line to get in. The classes filed into the hall for assembly.

The hall smelled strongly of cabbage and potatoes. Assembly consisted of prayers and a few notices from the head teacher. Finally, the children all trailed out with their form teachers and went to their classrooms.

Danny's form teacher was a Mrs Cartwright. While she took the register, Danny was told to stand by her desk. When she had finished calling the names she smiled and said, 'We have a new boy here today: Daniel Bailey. He's been living for two years in a place called Aden, a British colony which is on the bottom right hand corner of the Red Sea. Can you tell us a little bit about Aden, Daniel?'

Embarrassed and uncomfortable, Danny faced the class. Some of the boys were staring at him as if he had just come

from Mars. A girl in the front row was smiling in a friendly fashion. A dark-haired boy at the back was grinning.

'Well, it's – you see, my dad is in the air force and he was posted to Aden for two years. He's a mechanic on Meteor jets.'

Jets! The classroom buzzed for a moment. Rochford airport was nearby, but that only had aeroplanes with propellers.

Danny continued. 'Aden is just rocks and sand, really. It's surrounded by desert and sea. Aden's got a huge dead volcano in the middle. There's a whole town been built inside the volcano . . .'

Danny could have gone on for hours about Aden, about how the gazelles and pi-dogs came out of the desert and wandered the dusty streets. About the ragged-looking kite hawks which dropped from the sky and scavenged from the dustbins. How it was sweltering the whole year round and the children went swimming every single day. Talking about it made him feel very homesick for his

British and Arab friends who were still out there. He wanted to be back, under hard blue skies, camping at the weekends at Sheik Othman oasis, clambering over the forts left by the Moors, watching the sleek ocean liners leave Steamer Point harbour.

'. . . anyway, that's what it's like.'

'Thank you, Daniel,' said Mrs Cartwright. 'Would you take your place next to Paul Jackson.' She pointed to the desk next to the dark-haired grinning boy at the back. Danny went and sat next to the boy, who nodded in a friendly way.

'Jacko,' he said, introducing himself. 'Talk to you at break-time.'

'I have to see Mr Simpson then. Maybe later?'

At break-time, Danny had to ask three times for directions to Mr Simpson's room. Finally it was Jacko who told him where to go.

'Thanks,' said Danny. 'Catch you later.'

'Yeah - after school.'

When Danny got to Mr Simpson's class Robbo had already been ticked off.

'You're late,' said Mr Simpson.

'This is my first day,' complained Danny. 'I didn't know the way.'

'You've got a tongue in your head, haven't you?'

'And I used it, but it's still not easy, finding your way round a big place like this, sir.'

Mr Simpson stared at him for a

moment then nodded. 'Anyway, you're here now. I'm always saying we should assign an old pupil to a new one, as a guide. It would serve you both right if I appointed Robson to show you round.'

Danny and Robbo looked at the teacher in horror. He gave them a wry smile. 'Well, perhaps not.'

Both boys were then warned about fighting in the playground. Robbo received an additional warning about bullying, in or out of school. 'You have a reputation for bullying, Robson, and I'm telling you now, if I hear of any more of it you'll be up in front of the head. If that doesn't frighten you, I'll personally pay a visit to your father. You understand? No

more bullying. It's cowardly, especially against a new boy on his first day. It really wouldn't hurt you to show Danny round, but I'll leave that up to you.'

Robbo, who was not afraid of the headmaster but was terrified of his own father, nodded sullenly. However, he had no intention of helping Danny with the geography of the school. After they had left Mr Simpson's room, Robbo said, 'You just stay out of my way, new kid.'

'Suits me,' replied Danny. 'I didn't like that any more than you did, you know.'

'Yeah, well – just keep out of my way.'

2. New friends for old

As Danny walked home from school that evening he realised it was true what Mr Simpson had said. Every time he went to a new place he had to learn new maps. The school was a bewildering maze of corridors and classrooms and the nearest town and countryside were unfamiliar to him. The last time he had stayed with his grandparents he had been at primary school, just after the war, and he could hardly remember it.

Worst of all, he did not know where all

the kids gathered
outside school hours.
In the park? Down by
the abandoned river
mills? Behind the
village cricket
pavilion? There
would be a place
where they met and
talked and played

games, but where that place was would
remain a mystery to him until someone
told him or took him there.

'Yah, new kid!'

Several boys on bicycles swept past
him, one flicking his school satchel off his
shoulder. Robbo and his crew. They went

down the hill hooting over their shoulders. Then one of them stopped, turned, and came back. It was Jacko. He still had that wide grin on his face. Jacko was effervescent. He bubbled. Danny knew he would grow to like him.

'Wuppa, Danny,' said Jacko, using the local greeting. 'Where you going?'

'Home,' replied Danny. 'My nan's house. It's at the bottom of the hill. You one of Robbo's mates?'

'Nah. Just a whole bunch of us go home in the same direction. I live in a caravan down by the river. We're gypsies. Settled down now for a bit, though. Dad says he was gettin' dizzy, travelling round and round the country.'

enough money for a new one. Robbo started the craze. He's good at making things. French arrows, spoke-flicker cards, stuff like that. He's a bit of a pain sometimes. Gave me a hard time when I first got here. But he knows where the best rubbish dumps are. Things like that. Robbo knows where the best conker trees are in the conker season and where to scrump apples, and the best potato picking fields.'

Danny knew the Red Sea monsoon season, the box jellyfish season, and the shark season, but remembered very little about conkers or apples. He had known once, when he was nine, but that was a very long time ago. He had a vague idea they were both in the autumn. Potato picking? Spring or summer? That sounded like work, though in what month it took place he had no idea.

'Well, I don't like him.'

'And he don't like you, which makes

you even,' said Jacko, grinning. 'Hey, you want to come home with me? Meet my mum and dad, and my sister? Come and see our caravan. My mum'll cook us some sausages and chips.'

They went to check with Danny's grandparents first.

Danny's grandfather was the local chimney sweep and grave digger. Grandad Bailey had a horse and cart and often did not come back from work until quite late. Danny's grandmother was home, though. She was just putting out the fire under the copper, a big ceramic tub in which she did her washing. Electricity had not reached these country houses yet. There was gas lighting and a

J 103 030

wireless set run by a battery. She knew all about the gypsy site and agreed to let Danny visit Jacko's family.

'I think I've seen your mum on the bus once or twice,' said Nan to Jacko.

'S'pect so. She catches it further down the lane.'

'You be home before dark,' she said to Danny. 'You can lose track of time on these long summer evenings.'

'I will, Nan,' he replied, and the two boys set out for the river, which lay across three wide fields.

Jacko pushed his bike along the grass verge which tracked the hedgerow. On the way he pointed out various creatures in and around the ditches: rabbits, a stoat, a distant fox. He knew the names of all the trees and birds too. The gypsy boy was very knowledgeable about the countryside.

Danny was impressed. It was what he had missed about England when in Aden. Like Jacko, he loved the animals and birds of the fields and woods, the waterways.

The sound of church bells came drifting

over the fields as they reached the gyspy site. It reminded Danny that in Aden he would have been hearing *muezzins* calling Moslems to prayer from the tops of minarets at about this time. It was odd having to get used to different sounds, a different way of life. Even in the country of his birth things were strange to him. Inside, he was a mixture of two completely different lands and ways of life: one of them Moslem and one Christian.

Jacko's parents greeted Danny like a long lost son, saying he was the first school friend Jacko had brought home. Danny was soon tucking into egg, sausage and chips inside the colourful wooden caravan. Jacko's sister, a year younger than Danny, told him her name was Colly. She was very pretty in a wild sort of way, which made Danny a little shy. He did not know what to say to her, though this did not stop her chattering away about a pony she obviously adored.

'You like school, do you?' asked Jacko's dad. 'Me and the missis, we don't read, so it's good for us that Jacko and Colly do. We didn't get no schooling, see,' he explained, puffing on a briar pipe. 'No such thing when we was kids. Not for us gypsies, any rate.'

'Hard for us to settle down, until now,' said Jacko's mum. 'People chase us off. Farmers and such. Gyspies are not bad

people. They say we steal things, but not my family! There's good and bad everywhere.'

She had become a bit heated. Her dark eyes sparkled as she waved a weathered brown hand in front of Danny's face. Then she suddenly stopped and laughed. 'Nothin' to do with you, though, young Danny. All water under the bridge now. Did you like your chips?'

'Very nice, Mrs Jackson,' said Danny. 'When . . .' He stopped. He was about to say, 'When I was in Aden . . .' but he knew from experience that this phrase would mean nothing to most people. If repeated enough, it simply annoyed them. They had no idea what Aden was like and most did not want to know. 'When I get home,' he said, 'I'll tell Nan how well you looked after me.'

Afterwards, Jacko walked halfway home with Danny, to make sure he knew the way.

'Games tomorrow,' Jacko said, as they parted. 'Don't forget to dubbin your football boots.'

'I haven't got any football boots.'

'Well, never mind, most of us play in plimsoles. Hey, which team do you support? Do you know . . .' and here Jacko went into a stream of words, listing clubs, his favourite players, names of venues. Danny's heart sank. Here was something else he did not know about.

Football. It had been too hot for soccer in Aden. There they had only played cricket, and swam. And England had been three weeks away by ship. Newspapers, magazines, letters – they were all nearly a month out of date when they arrived in Aden. Consequently they had not been of much interest to Danny and his friends, living under a tropical sun.

Now he was going to have to admit to ignorance again. It didn't matter with Jacko. Danny felt they shared a common bond: they both belonged to families which moved around a lot. Jacko wouldn't laugh at him, but Robbo would, without a doubt.

Danny laughed. 'Really? Where d'you get the bike?'

'This?' Jacko looked down proudly at his machine. It had huge 'cow-horn' handlebars. 'Made it. Got a paper round and used the money to buy the brakes and pedals and things. The frame comes from a rubbish dump. And the saddle's from a postman's bike. One of my uncles gave me that. Really springy. Wanna try it out?'

Danny climbed on to the comfortable saddle and rode up and down, before handing the machine back to his new friend.

'Great, are all the bikes handmade?'

'Most of 'em. No one round here's got

3. Missing

Next day at school, some news was buzzing around the playground.

'What's up?' asked Danny of Jacko.

'An old woman's gone missing from her cottage,' said Jacko. 'Been gone three days now. It was in last night's local paper. Police are out looking for her.'

'How do they know?'

'They found her car in Horseshoe Lane.'

'A car? She must be rich.'

'Yep, well, a neighbour saw her drive off

with her Yorkshire terrier, but there's no old lady and no dog in the car. They reckon she's been murdered. Or fallen in the river or something. No one's seen her since.'

The bell went for assembly and Danny had to wait to hear more. That afternoon Jacko happily went off to football, but Danny asked if he could go to cricket practice. He was quite a good bowler and a medium batsman, but he knew he would have to prove himself yet again to a new games' master. When Danny asked for a trial for the school team the games' master seemed irritable.

'What do you want a trial for?'

'Because I think I'm good enough to

get into the school team.'

'But you've only been here five minutes!'

'Sir, that doesn't mean I'm no good. I was in my last school team.'

'And where was that?' asked the teacher. 'Harrow or Eton?'

Danny ignored the sarcasm. 'Khormaksar School, Aden.'

'Never heard of it.'

'I'd never heard of Rochford School, until I came here,' remarked Danny, hotly.

'Don't you get cheeky with me, my lad.'

Now Danny knew he would have to prove himself doubly good to get anywhere near the school cricket team.

He made a reasonable showing in the

nets a few moments later, but only when he came to bowl did he reveal any real flair for the game. He noticed the games' master watching him out of the corner of his eye, but nothing was said after cricket practice was over. Danny was bitterly disappointed.

Afterwards, in the changing-rooms, Danny and Jacko spoke more about the missing woman.

'Have you heard?' whispered Jacko. 'The police have asked Robbo to help them with their inquiries.'

Danny stopped feeling sorry for himself. 'You mean they've nicked him for a crime?'

'No, no,' Jacko said impatiently. 'That

missing woman thing. Robbo's lived here all his life. He knows the marshes like the backs of his hands. They want him to show them all the hidey holes, where she might have fallen. Whatever.'

'Really?' replied Danny, impressed. 'Couldn't you do that? You're a gypsy. You know places.'

'Nah, I'm a bit like you. I only stop in one place long enough to take a quick breath, then we move again.'

The two boys were envious of Robbo. They had a grudging admiration for someone who knew the marshes so well. They would have liked to have been the ones to show the police over everywhere. It was a position of importance. Robbo

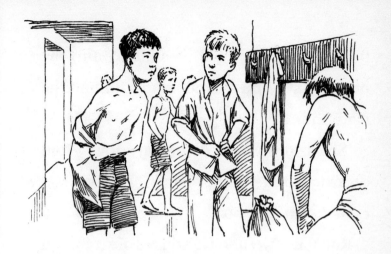

became impossible to live with, too. He strutted round the changing-room, telling everyone about his new post as police guide. They didn't even blame him for that. Danny and Jacko would have felt just as proud of themselves if they had been asked to help the police.

'They're goin' to use dogs, of course, to sniff out her trail – but you've got to show dogs where to look in the first place, ain't ya? Otherwise they'll be sniffing into the next county and still no nearer finding the woman.'

'She's probably dead by now,' said Stocky, wonderingly. 'You'll have to see a dead body, Robbo.'

Robson went slightly pale for a moment, but the colour soon came back to his face. 'Well, if I do, it's all for the good, ain't it? It's somethin' that's just got to be done.'

While they were walking home, Jacko wheeling his bike and Danny kicking a stone along the gutter, both boys were deep in thought.

'I bet we could find her,' said Danny at last. 'We could get some Ordnance

Survey maps from the library.'

'What are they?'

'They're the best maps you can get. I was in the scouts in Aden. We were taught to read Ordnance Survey maps. What say we get one?'

'Wouldn't the police have them?'

Danny nodded. 'Oh yes, but you've got to know a *bit* about the countryside too. You know all that kind of stuff, Jacko, about where the warmest place is out of the wind, and the driest, and what things a person would find to eat in the wild. What do you say? Tomorrow's the weekend. Let's go on a search, a quest, like knights looking for the Holy Grail.'

'Holy *girl*, you mean,' said Jacko

seriously.

Danny laughed uproariously. He knew it was going to be more difficult than usual to say goodbye to the gyspy boy when the time came. They both had a lot in common. They had a love of nature and the countryside, where they could let their imaginations loose.

Robbo was of a similar mind: but he also had a nasty streak in his character which made him more of a rival than anything else. Now Danny was determined to find the woman before Robbo did.

That night Danny lay in his bed, staring up into the darkness, thinking about the problem. He tried to imagine what might happen to a person out in a marshy area. They might fall foul of some murderer, they might die of something sudden like a heart attack, they might drown. These were all possibilities. However, if the woman was dead, why hadn't the dog turned up somewhere? What if the woman had fallen into a deep hole, say a bomb crater from the war, and couldn't get out? The dog might be in the hole too, or refuse to leave her? It might be a battle against time to get to her before she did die!

4. The search begins

'What's she doing here?' asked Danny, more out of surprise than anything else.

Colly glowered at him. 'Jacko told me what you're doing. I want to come too. I can read maps, see.'

'Didn't say you couldn't,' murmured Danny, feeling put down. 'Just arskin', that's all.'

Colly's presence put Danny in a bit of a tizz. Girls were a mystery to him. It was not that he disliked them, but their ideas often flew in a completely different

direction to his own. They seemed to think sideways, and when you were on a mission as important as this one, you wanted someone who agreed with all your suggestions. Otherwise you spent half the day arguing.

It was late Saturday morning. Most kids were at the cattle market in Rochford Square and there was no one else around.

They spread the map, which Danny had got from the local library, on the floorboards of the cricket pavilion verandah. They studied the terrain of Rochford and its surrounds. Even before looking at the map they knew it was a salt marsh area, with tidal rivers and flat islands covered in poa grass, bladderwort and sea lavender. Now, as they studied the contours of the land, they could see that there were only one or two shallow hills, and the rest was flatlands. Unless the missing woman had been sucked down in some bog, Danny could not imagine where she would be hidden.

'Here's where the car was found,' he pointed out. 'Look, there's a footpath

right by it. I bet she took her dog for a walk down there.'

Colly remarked, 'The newspaper already said that.'

'Well,' Danny argued, irritated that she had started on him already, 'I'm just going over the facts. If you look at where the footpath goes, it ends on the river bank. Did the paper say that, too?'

'No.'

'Then there's something we know that others don't.'

Jacko said, 'Stop fighting, you two. Listen, I've just thought of something. The dog.'

'Dog?' repeated Danny, who had never had a pet. It wasn't practical for a family who moved so often. 'What about it?'

Jacko explained. 'The woman had a dog with her, didn't she? Well, even if she had an accident or was murdered, the dog would still be alive. I mean, it might have been killed by the murderer, but it's more likely it ran off.'

'So?'

'So, where is it?' cried Jacko triumphantly. 'It's not turned up anywhere.'

'I bet she's dead,' said Colly so matter-of-factly it turned Danny's blood cold. 'I bet she's lying in some peat hollow in the marshes right now and her faithful hound is still by her side. He's sitting there, waiting for someone to find his mistress.'

'Exactly,' cried Jacko, and he and his sister exchanged significant looks.

Danny was still as mystified as ever. 'How's this going to help us?' he said. 'I still don't understand. If the dog's still sitting there, then we've got to find them both at once. So nothing's changed.'

Colly laughed. 'Course it has. Dogs need to drink, don't they? Even if they can go without food for days they need fresh water. These are the salt marshes. The river is sea water, flowing in from the Channel.'

Suddenly a great veil lifted from Danny's mind. 'I get it. What we have to do is find out where the dog is getting fresh water from!' Determined not to be outdone by the other two, he studied the map. Back in Aden, water sellers were as numerous on the streets as newspaper boys were in England. They charged for their water by the small cupful. Having lived in a land where water is a rare and precious commodity, Danny thought of deep wells and collecting-tanks for rainwater. He had lived near such tanks in Aden: the Queen of Sheba's wells.

Deep wells, like those built in England, would be no good to a thirsty dog. The hound would not be able to reach the water to drink from it. Danny got the answer straight away, even as he stared at the crazed pattern of marshes and backwaters.

'Ponds! Dew ponds!' he said. 'They're collecting-tanks for the rain in places where there's no water for cattle or sheep. Usually you find them on hills and downland. Do the farmers have cattle round here?'

'Yes,' replied Colly excitedly. 'They

graze their animals on the salt marsh islands in the summer. They cross the river on tracks called 'hards' when the tide is out. You can see the tracks marked by witches' brooms, stuck upside down in the mud. Occasionally hunters get lost out on the mud, shooting Brent geese. Then rescuers set light to the brush bits on the brooms, so the lost person can see their way to a hard.'

'Right,' said Danny, fascinated by what Colly said, but not willing to admit it. 'Well, they'll need fresh water for the cattle over there on the islands, which probably means building dew ponds to collect the rain water.'

'There'll be rabbits and other wildlife

around a fresh water pond – which would mean food for the dog to catch,' said Jacko.

They studied the Ordnance Survey map and found several dew ponds marked on various islands in the estuary. It was a race against Robbo and the police to find the woman first. Danny was determined it should be Colly, Jacko and himself that found her. Absolutely determined.

5. The rivals

Over the next day or so, the three friends roamed the local creeks – Lion Creek, Brandy Hole, Ballards Gore – searching for dew ponds and a dog's pawprints, which they called 'spoor'. Colly and Jacko were good at finding and identifying spoor and they taught Danny to do the same. At first the gypsy pair made fun of Danny's poor efforts, but when he asked them the difference between the prints of a gazelle and those of a Damascus goat, they realised they did not know everything about animal tracks. When Colly said she was amazed that Danny had never ridden a horse, he said he was equally astonished that she had never been on the back of a dromedary camel. They both laughed and called it quits.

Their searches were all in vain. They found plenty of fox prints, hare prints, those of a wildcat or two, but few belonging to dogs. Those they did find were not the spoor which would be left by a Yorkshire terrier.

Back at school, Robbo was still showing off and bragging about being a police 'guide'. In the end, Jacko could stand it no longer.

'Listen, we're looking for the woman too – me, Danny and Colly – and we'll find her before *you* ever do.'

'Oh, yeah?' cried Robbo. 'Well, you better watch it, you dirty little tinker, because mine's the *official* search, see. You'll get into trouble if you start nosin' around where you're not wanted.'

'And *you'll* get into even more trouble, Robson,' said an eavesdropping Mr

Simpson, 'if ever I hear you call anyone "a dirty little tinker" again. We'll have no bigots in this school. See me in my room after classes.'

'*After classes?*' cried Robbo. 'There's a school soccer match right after school – I *am* the school goalie, I hope you know, sir.'

'You don't seem to realise the seriousness of your offence, boy! Would you rather I took this to your father? I now want you to apologise to Jackson for your stupid name-calling.'

Robbo went white during Mr Simpson's tirade. He had never seen the master so angry before. Even some of the kids were looking at Robbo strangely. Robson was a boy who, because of his troubled home life, liked being popular around the school.

'Yes, sir,' he whispered, hoarsely. 'Detention then.'

Robbo walked away, sulking. Jacko knew they had made a dangerous enemy, but he also knew that if his parents had heard he had been called names – tinker, pikey, diddycoy – they would be down to the school and yelling blue murder. He said as much to Danny.

Danny replied, 'You know, when I first went to Aden I was at a school where there were nearly all Arab children and only a few British kids. No one ever called me names there. It's something we do here which I don't like.'

The evenings were long and pleasant. Beautiful red skies, sometimes streaked with thin clouds like mackerel stripes, continued to parade themselves through the rest of the week. Dragonflies hung

suspended over the marshes, like little chips of blue stone. Midges formed dark smoky swarms over the muddy banks of the creeks.

Danny, Colly and Jacko were more determined than ever to find the missing woman before Robbo did. It became a point of honour. Robbo now knew they were looking too, and his own search became more intense and important to him. He would not look good to the local kids if a stranger to their school found the woman before he did.

The explorations took the three friends to various islands, to which they could walk at low tide, though they sometimes sank into the grey, foul-smelling mud up

to their knees. Finally they were left with only one or two islands where the ooze was really too deep to risk crossing by foot. The only way to reach these islands was to swim.

'It has to be at high tide, when the currents are weakest,' said Colly. 'If the tide is on the ebb or the flow, a person will get taken down to the mill sluices one

way, or out into the open sea the other.'

'You mean they'll drown,' Danny said flatly.

'That's what she means,' confirmed Jacko. 'Colly is right – it's a dangerous business, swimming out to those islands.'

Danny asked, 'What does the tide table say?'

Colly replied, 'High tide tomorrow is at

six in the evening.'

Danny stared at the wide stretch of water across the creek. It was a quarter of a mile to the far bank. He could make such a distance easily. In Aden he had swum in the two-mile race every year. Colly and Jacko were not good swimmers, he knew, and any stretch of water looked dangerous to them.

'I'll do it tomorrow,' he told the other two, 'dead on six o'clock.'

Colly showed the worry in her eyes.

'Danny,' she said, 'I don't want you to do this. It's too far. You don't know what eddies and currents are out there. You might get swept round the headland before you know it. Please don't do it.'

He smiled at this dark-eyed, serious sister of his new friend, knowing that soon all of them would have to part. All three were used to saying goodbye to people. Danny always took these sad moments in his stride, hoping that one day they would meet up again. Now was the first time in his life that he had felt old enough to keep a promise to write letters, keep in touch, perhaps make *sure* that the 'one day' he always spoke about would be more than just a possibility. After all, Colly and Jacko would be sure to camp on the gypsy site again sometime. And if he knew when, Danny could visit his grandparents' house at the same time. He need never let go of *these* two pals.

'I'll be all right,' he assured her. 'I swam in the Red Sea every day in Aden, even in the monsoon season when there were waves as high as houses. I'm the best swimmer you've ever seen. I can cut through the water like a shark.'

'John Robson is the best swimmer I've ever seen,' she said, astonishing him with her reply. 'I think you're just bragging to stop me worrying about you.'

6. Jay Island's secret

The following day at precisely six o'clock, Danny was standing on the bank of the river in his swimming-trunks. Colly was there, looking concerned. Jacko, who had complete faith in his friend's ability to

swim the stretch of water, stood by with a towel. The three had arrived at about five-thirty, but had hidden when they saw the police with their dogs around the abandoned mills, just half a mile away. Robbo had been with them, clearly evident from his red shirt, which was like a flag announcing his presence. Then the police had vanished in their van and the coast was clear.

Out in deeper water, moored yachts were pointing in all directions. There was no strong flow either way. They were just drifting idly on still water.

'Well, here goes,' said Danny, preparing to dive in. 'Wish me luck!'

At that moment Robbo appeared out of

the bushes, with Stocky.

'Wha' d'you think you're doin'?' Robbo asked.

'I'm swimming out to Jay Island, to see if the old woman is there.' Danny saw no reason to keep secrets from Robbo now. 'We worked out there's a dew pond over there, which would keep her dog alive.'

Robbo's eyes narrowed. 'You reckon, do you?'

'Yes, we do.'

'And you're goin' to swim it?'

'Yes, I am.'

Robbo said, 'I've done that swim a dozen times. I'm the only one at our school that's done it so far. I've not got me trunks on though. You think you can do it? Let's see you, new kid.'

Colly said to him, 'Have you really swum it?'

The youth turned and looked at Colly as if she were an ant. When she lifted her

chin defiantly and stared back with hard eyes, he decided it would be better to answer her. 'I said so, didn't I?' he replied, quietly.

'I've seen him,' Stocky cried, rushing to the defence of his leader. 'What, are you callin' Robbo a liar?'

'Leave it alone, Stocky,' said Robbo. 'Let's see how the Olympic swimmer does.'

Danny stood on the muddy bank of the creek. On the other side of the water a hawk hovered over the island. It was a still evening, with few waves on the water. Then Danny dived in and began swimming towards the far bank. The others watched him cutting through the water, noting the smooth overarm strokes.

'You sure he ain't an Australian?' Robbo said, with grudging admiration. 'He knows nothin' about football, he's only half-good at cricket, but he can swim all right . . .'

While the other four watched him, Danny reached the middle of the river in quick time. It was colder in the centre and the current was indeed stronger there, but since it was high tide there was no rapid flow. Once the tide began to ebb, then the water would start to flow swiftly towards the ocean.

When he reached Jay Island, Danny turned and gave his watchers a little wave. Then he began walking along the shoreline, which was formed of many small creeks and inlets. On its edges the greater island was made up of smaller islands. Danny searched along the shoreline until he came to a place where the grass was trodden down. There were a dog's paw marks all round the area.

'Yes!' whispered Danny to himself.

'The dog's here.'

There were a few stunted trees in this area and quite a few elder bushes. After a further search he found a rough path through the poa grass. It took Danny a lot of courage to follow that track. The missing woman had been gone for a week now. Everyone was saying she would be dead. Danny was not looking forward to seeing a dead person. He was full of dread. He walked slowly, so as not to be surprised by the body. He did not want to find it by tripping over it.

It was the dog he saw first, darting towards him. When it reached him the little animal leaped up full of excitement on to Danny's chest. Its scrabbling claws scratched his skin. He held the wriggling terrier and let it lick his face a dozen times. It seemed full of joy to see him. It could not keep still, dropping to the ground, running round and through his legs several times, then jumping up again, yapping and panting.

'All right, boy – careful,' Danny said. 'Calm down.'

Then Danny heard a faint cry from behind a brake of bracken and blackberry bushes. The woman was alive! He ran towards the spot where the sound had come from, with the dog close on his heels.

She was lying on her side, near to a dew pond which was nothing more than a rough hollow square lined with bricks. Her face was gaunt and pale, her summer dress hung from her bones. It was obvious she had lost a lot of weight over the last few days.

'Thank God you've come,' she croaked. 'I was beginning to give up hope. I've hurt my ankle.'

Even now Danny felt helpless to do anything. He moved forward, but she held up a hand. 'You can't carry me,' she said. 'Go and get help. I'll be fine now I know help is on the way.'

'All right.'

He ran back to the river again. The moored yachts now had their bows pointing up river. Since the mooring ropes

were attached to buoys from the prows of the yachts, this meant there was a strong flow down river towards the sea. The tide had turned again! Danny stared at the water, knowing it would be foolish and dangerous to attempt the return crossing. Instead, he ran back to the place where he had climbed out and signalled to his friends on the far bank.

'Hi!' he yelled. 'She's here! She's over here. Still alive.'

Even as he called he knew they could not hear him. He jumped up and down, waving like mad, pointing back to where the woman lay. Finally, after several charades, they seemed to grasp what he was trying to convey. Robbo and Stocky ran off, presumably to fetch someone. Colly and Jacko remained on the far bank. Danny appreciated this. He would have felt abandoned if they had all gone away.

He ran back to the woman now. She told him she had taken a rowing boat out to Jay Island to do some blackberrying. Her eyes were dark round the edges and she looked close to fainting, but she insisted on talking to him. She said she had been alone for too long.

'No one comes over here and the bushes are full of fruit,' she said. 'The boat belongs to some neighbours of mine. They're in Spain for the whole summer and they said I could use it. There was nowhere to tie it up, so I used a mooring stake, but when I came back in the evening the tide had pulled the boat loose. I got a bit frightened when I knew I had to spend the night here, after the tide had gone out. In the darkness I stumbled and hurt my ankle. I think it's broken . . .'

She showed Danny an ugly swollen foot.

'. . . I managed to crawl here, to the pool, so I had water. A series of accidents, really.'

'Didn't you have anything to eat?'

'Oh, I ate all the blackberries.' She managed to laugh, even though she was obviously in pain. 'And any elderberries I could reach.'

Danny stayed with her until he heard shouts. Then he stood up and hurried to fetch the rescuers. The dog weaved in and out of his legs as he ran, over-excited and liable to trip him up at any moment.

Danny led the police to the woman, who immediately broke down and started crying.

Embarrassed by this emotional outburst, Danny allowed himself to be led to a dinghy with an outboard motor. He was taken back across the river, allowed to dress and, after a few questions, was taken home by a policewoman. He did not even have the chance to talk to his friends.

Danny's grandmother told him off for

swimming across the river, then hugged him and said he had saved the woman's life. She gave him a cup of cocoa and settled him in an armchair. Then she told him, 'You've got to go back to your mum and dad in two days.'

Nan looked a bit upset, but Danny wasn't sure whether this was because of the swim or because he had to leave.

It seemed his father had been posted suddenly to Singapore. The ship was leaving in two weeks.

'Your mum's coming to get you on Tuesday.'

Danny took the news in his stride. He was used to such surprises. That night he went to bed with a warm glow in his heart.

On Monday he was standing in the playground when he heard a familiar cry.

'Hey, new kid!'

He turned to see a grinning Robbo striding towards him.

'We did it, eh? We found that old woman and her dog. The head's going to announce it in front of the whole school today. An' the woman's going to take us all to Southend for a treat, when she's better. You, me and Jacko and his sister, too. What d'you think?'

Danny didn't resent Robbo getting some attention too. He recognised that Robbo had given up hours of his time to help in the search. And, in the end, everyone knew it was Danny who found the woman, with Jacko and Colly's help.

'Good,' replied Danny, smiling. 'Only I can't make it.'

Robbo was taken aback. 'Why not?'

'Moving on again. My mum's coming
to fetch me tomorrow. Anyway, you'll
be able to go.'

Robbo shrugged. 'Yeah. Where're you
goin'?'

'R.A.F. Changi. It's in Singapore.'

'You want to watch it. There's some weird people out in those places,' said Robbo, seriously.

But unknown lands held no fears for Danny. He had been to such places before and found that the people in foreign places were much like they were anywhere else. They had a different way of life, but that was something to look forward to, something exciting. Once he got there, Danny would have to make new friendships, learn new maps, break new ground at a new school, prove himself over again. But that was to be expected. At least in Singapore there would be others like him.

That evening he said goodbye to Colly and Jacko.

'Be on our way some time ourselves, I bet,' said Jacko.

'Try not to get dizzy again,' said Danny, grinning.

Colly said, 'And you – don't forget to write to me. No one's ever written a letter to me before. I'll be looking forward to it.'

'Hey,' cried Jacko, mounting his bike, 'we got our pictures in the local paper. We're famous, we are!'

Danny watched them ride away, a lump in his throat, and anticipation in his heart. He felt a little light headed. There was a long sea voyage ahead of him. Six weeks at least. Then tropical climes and a new way of life. It was enough to make anyone giddy with excitement. He had just helped to solve one mystery – the riddle of the missing woman – and now he was set for more discoveries in new mysterious lands.

If you enjoyed this
MAMMOTH READ try:

Badger Boy

Anthony Masters
Illustrated by Joan-Marie Abley

Barry has withdrawn into his own world.
Now he only has time for the badgers that
live in the nearby wood.

His cousin Kerry is desperate to be his
friend. But how can she get through to him?

Then the new farmer threatens to clear the
wood. Barry's badgers will be homeless.

Is this a battle he can fight on his own?